ZONDERKIDZ

The Berenstain Bears® Treasury
Copyright © 2012 by Berenstain Bears, Inc.
Illustrations © 2012 by Berenstain Bears, Inc.

Requests for information should be addressed to:
Zonderkidz, Grand Rapids, Michigan 49530

ISBN 978-0-310-60522-5

The Berenstain Bears® and the Golden Rule ISBN 9780310712473 (2008)
The Berenstain Bears® Go to Sunday School ISBN 9780310712480 (2008)
The Berenstain Bears® Forgiving Tree ISBN 9780310720843 (2011)
The Berenstain Bears® Say Their Prayer ISBN 9780310712466 (2008)
The Berenstain Bears® Faithful Friends ISBN 9780310712534 (2009)
The Berenstain Bears® Show Some Respect ISBN 9780310720867 (2011)
The Berenstain Bears® Kindness Counts ISBN 9780310712572 (2010)
The Berenstain Bears® and a Job Well Done ISBN 9780310712541 (2010)

Editor: Mary Hassinger
Cover and interior design: Cindy Davis

Printed in China

12 13 14 15 16 17 18 19 /LPC/ 10 9 8 7 6 5 4 3 2 1

The Berenstain Bears®

Living Lights™

Treasury

written by
Jan & Mike Berenstain

The Berenstain Bears
and the Golden Rule

Bear Country School

Created by Stan and Jan Berenstain
Written by Mike Berenstain

ZONDERVAN.com/
AUTHORTRACKER
follow your favorite authors

ZONDERkidz

When Sister Bear received a beautiful golden locket for her birthday, she was surprised and pleased. It was shaped like a heart, and it had her name on it.

"Happy birthday, dear!" said Mama and Papa Bear, giving her a big hug.

Sister tried the locket on and looked at herself in the mirror. "I love it!" she said. "I'm going to wear it all the time."

"It opens up," said Papa. "Look!" He showed her the little golden clasp that you pressed to pop the locket open.

"Neat!" said Sister.

She looked inside, expecting to find a little picture or a mirror or something. But all that she could see inside the locket were a few simple words: "Do to others what you would have them do to you."

Sister was puzzled. The words seemed familiar. But she wasn't sure why. "What's this?" she asked.

"It's the golden rule," explained Mama.

"What's that?" Sister wondered.

Mama's eyes widened. "The golden rule is one of the most important rules there is," she explained. "That's why we have always had it hanging up on the wall of our living room." She pointed to the framed sampler above their mantelpiece.

Sister gazed up at it in amazement. She had seen that sampler every day of her life. No wonder the words seemed familiar! "Oh," she said, a little embarrassed. "I never really thought about what it said before. What does it mean?"

"The golden rule," Papa explained, "tells you to treat other people the way you want to be treated yourself."

"Why is it inside my locket?" she wondered.

"It's a *golden* rule inside a *golden* locket for a little *golden* princess!" said Papa, giving her a big kiss.

"It's called the golden rule," explained Mama, patiently, "because it's precious, just like gold. But it's not about the gold you wear around your neck or on your finger." She held out her wedding ring. "It's about the golden treasure we keep inside our own hearts. The heart shape of the locket is meant to remind you of that."

Sister thought it over. She didn't really get it. But that was okay. She loved the new locket anyway.

The next day before school, Sister showed off her new
treasure to her friends Lizzy, Millie, Anna, and Linda.
They oohed and ahhed over it in a very satisfying way.
"What's all the fuss about?" asked a voice.

It was Queenie McBear and her gang. Queenie was older than Sister and a little snooty. When Queenie first came to the neighborhood, she and Sister did not get along at all. Queenie made fun of her and got Sister's friends to join in. That was Sister's first experience with an in-crowd—a group that makes itself feel big by making others feel small.

"Oh, hi Queenie," said Sister. "I was just showing the kids my new locket."

Over the years, Sister learned to get along with Queenie. But they never were the best of friends.

"Let's see!" said Queenie.

She looked the locket over. She was not impressed. She herself wore big hoop earrings and lots of beads and chains.

"Cute," was all she said as she walked away with her friends.

Queenie still had her own in-crowd. They were a group of the older girls who liked hanging out together and acting cool. Mostly, they spent their time painting their nails and giggling about boys.

That was okay with Sister. She had her own group of friends to hang out with. But it never occurred to her that this might be any kind of problem until the new girl came to school.

Her name was Suzy MacGrizzie. It seemed like a funny sort of name. For one thing, it had a lot of Zs in it. The new girl herself seemed a little funny too. Her clothes weren't exactly cool, and she wore her hair up in pigtails, which was definitely not the standard Bear Country School style. Besides, she had thick glasses and braces—not the cool kind with lots of different colors like Millie wore—just plain old braces.

On her first day, of course, the new girl didn't know
anyone at all. At recess, Sister noticed her standing off
by herself in a corner of the playground. She looked sort
of sad and lonely. Sister was thinking about going over
and introducing herself when Lizzy and Anna came up.

"Hiya, Sister!" said Lizzy. "We're getting together a game of hopscotch. Millie and Linda are over there. Come on!"

Sister began to follow them. But she paused and glanced back to where the new girl was standing all by herself. The new girl looked lonelier than ever.

"Wait a minute," said Sister. "What about that new girl—that what's-her-name—the one over there? Maybe we should invite her to join in. She looks pretty lost and lonely."

The other girls were surprised.

"Suzy Whoozy-face?" said Lizzy, doubtfully.

"She has weird clothes," said Anna.

"And those corny pigtails," said Lizzy.

"Not to mention those clunky glasses and braces," added Anna.

"Well," said Sister, discouraged, "I just thought …"

"Oh, don't worry about old Suzy MacWhoozy!" said Lizzy, taking Sister's arm. "She'll be fine. She'll find some other cubs to play with—cubs more her type. Come on!"

Sister allowed herself to be led away to the hopscotch game. She felt a little worried about Suzy MacWhoozy, though she couldn't exactly say why. But she soon forgot all about it while playing hopscotch with her friends.

Later, when school let out, Sister got in line for her school bus. She noticed that the new girl was standing right in front of her. She was going to say hi, but then Lizzy came up behind her, and they started to talk. They went on talking as they got on the bus.

Suzy MacGrizzie sat right behind them. Sister and Lizzy went right on talking together. Sister played with her new locket as she talked, twirling it around and around in the air.

When the bus came to her stop, Sister gathered up her things to get off. But she felt a soft tug at her arm. It was Suzy MacGrizzie. She was holding something out to Sister.

"Here," she said shyly. "You dropped this." It was Sister's new locket!

"Gee," said Sister. "Thanks!" It was all she could think of to say.

Sister climbed off the bus and watched as it pulled away. She could see Suzy looking back at her from the window. Sister hung her locket back around her neck. What if Suzy hadn't noticed her drop it? It might have been gone for good.

Mama was waiting for Sister as she climbed the front steps. "How was school today, dear?" asked Mama.

"Oh, okay, I guess," sighed Sister, dumping her schoolbag on the armchair in the living room. She glanced up at the framed sampler of the golden rule over the mantel.

Somehow, the golden locket hanging around her neck felt heavier than before.

That evening at dinner, Sister was unusually thoughtful. She picked at her lima beans and stared off into space.

"A penny for your thoughts," said Papa as he fed Honey Bear.

"Huh?" said Sister, looking up. "Oh, I was just thinking about that golden rule inside my locket," she explained. "I don't really get it. What's it supposed to mean?"

"Well," began Mama. "Let me give you an example. Do you remember that trouble you had when Queenie first moved to town?"

Sister perked up and paid attention. She remembered it all too well.

"Do you remember how Queenie started an in-crowd but kept you out and made fun of your clothes and hair bow?" Mama asked. "Do you remember how badly you felt?"

Boy, did she ever! Sister started to feel hurt just thinking about it. Her lower lip began to quiver, and a tear came to her eye.

"All the golden rule is saying," Papa continued, "is that you shouldn't turn around and do that same sort of thing to someone else."

He paused to scrape some mashed potatoes off Honey's chin. "You should always treat other people the way you would like to be treated yourself."

"But I would never do anything like that!" said Sister. "Besides, I don't have an in-crowd."

"Oh no?" said Brother, who had been taking all this in. "What about Lizzy and Anna and Millie and Linda? You play with them all the time. But I never see you asking anyone else to join in!"

"That's different!" protested Sister, angrily. "I'm just playing with my friends! We're not trying to keep anybody out!"

"Of course not, dear!" soothed Mama. "I'm sure you and your friends would never dream of keeping other cubs out of your group."

Sister Bear grew very quiet. Now that she thought it over, she wasn't quite so sure—not so sure at all!

The next day at recess, as soon as Sister came outside, she looked around the playground for Suzy MacGrizzie. She soon spotted her, sitting off by herself under the big oak tree at the edge of the schoolyard and reading a book.

Sister marched right up to her. "Hello, Suzy!" she said brightly.

Suzy looked up in surprise. "Hello," she said shyly.

"I'm Sister Bear, and my friends and I are going to play some hopscotch," Sister told her. "Would you like to join us?"

Suzy's face lit up. "Oh, I'd love to!" she said with a big bracey grin. "I love hopscotch!"

"Terrific!" said Sister. "Do you want to see my locket?"

"Sure!" said Suzy.

"Okay," said Sister. "Come on! I'll show it to you … over there."

Sister took off, and Suzy chased her, laughing, across the playground to the hopscotch square where Lizzy, Millie, Anna, and Linda were waiting.

Sister's golden locket gleamed in the sun as she ran.

The Berenstain Bears®
Go to
Sunday
School

Created by Stan and Jan Berenstain
Written by Mike Berenstain

ZONDERkidz

ZONDERVAN.com/
AUTHORTRACKER
follow your favorite authors

Sunday morning was a busy time in the big tree house down a sunny dirt road deep in Bear Country. The Bear family had things to do and places to go. Brother had soccer practice at ten thirty, and Sister had a ballet lesson at eleven. Usually Mama dropped them off before taking Honey Bear along to do some grocery shopping. Papa stayed home to get his fix-up chores done early so he could watch football in the afternoon.

But it hadn't always been that way for the Bear family. A few years back, before they'd gotten involved with so many activities, the Bear family had gone every Sunday morning to services at the Chapel in the Woods. Of course, that meant Brother and Sister went to Sunday school.

Mama Bear missed those days. It seemed to her that the family was a lot closer back then. Going to the Chapel in the Woods was like a kind of glue that held the whole family together.

Mama decided it was time for a little family conference. They all gathered in the living room one Saturday night, and she told them what was on her mind.

"Glue?" said Sister, puzzled. "You mean like when you glued that lamp back together after we broke it?"

"That's a very good example," said Papa. "That lamp gave us light. We glued it back together so we wouldn't be left in the dark. Worshiping God gives us light and warmth too. And our family needs a little glue from time to time to keep it together."

Sister and Brother thought that one over. It made sense … sort of.

"Besides," said Mama, "I believe that going to church together is more important than all our other Sunday morning activities combined."

"More important than soccer?" gasped Brother, shocked.

"Or ballet?" chimed in Sister.

"Yes," Mama nodded firmly. "But don't get too excited. We'll go to the early service at eight thirty. That way, you'll have plenty of time to get to your soccer and ballet."

"Eight thirty in the morning?" cried Brother and Sister, even more upset. "That means we'll have to get up at seven o'clock—on the weekend!"

"Now, now," said Papa. He prided himself on always getting up early. "Early to bed and first to get up, makes a bear healthy, wealthy and … uh … how does that go?"

"Sleepy!" said Brother.

At breakfast the next morning, the Bear family did seem sleepy indeed. At least Brother and Sister did. They could hardly keep their eyes open. Papa wasn't exactly all there either. He was almost invisible behind his Sunday paper.

"Coffee, dear?" asked Mama, lifting the coffee pot.

"Uh!" grunted Papa, holding his cup out without looking up.

"Ahem!" said Mama.

"Huh—wha?" asked Papa, looking up. "Oh, sorry, my dear!" he said, folding the paper. "I guess I'm not really awake until I've had my morning coffee."

After breakfast, Mama put on her best Sunday hat. They climbed down the front steps, and Papa put Honey Bear in her stroller. The whole family headed down the road to the Chapel in the Woods.

Other families joined them as they walked along. There were their neighbors Farmer and Mrs. Ben. They saw Uncle Willie, Aunt Min, and Cousin Fred from down the street.

They even ran into Too-Tall Grizzly being hauled along by his parents, Two-Ton and Too-Too Grizzly.

The Chapel in the Woods was nestled in a pretty little glen down by the creek. On this fresh spring morning, the dogwoods were in bloom. Papa began to hum a tune. Then he started to sing, "Come to the church by the wildwood. Oh, come to the church in the vale."

Mama joined in, "No spot is so dear to my childhood ..."

They finished together, "As the little brown church in the vale."

"What weird song is that?" asked Sister.

"Oh, it's just something we used to sing in church, together, when we were children," sighed Mama. "That was a long time ago."

"Did you know each other way back then?" asked Brother.

"Know each other!" laughed Papa. "Why, I was sweet on your mother when we were only eight years old. She was the cutest cub in the whole Sunday school. Once, I brought a frog into class. I was going to let it loose during the story of the plagues of Egypt. But I decided it would be funnier to slip it down Mama's back—it was too!"

Brother's and Sister's eyes widened, imagining the scene. "Wow!" they breathed softly.

"Now, dear," said Mama. "Let's not give the children any bright ideas."

They dropped Honey Bear off at the church nursery and filed quietly into the chapel. There was soft music playing on the organ as they found a pew. Then Preacher Brown climbed into the pulpit, and the service began.

"Welcome, friends!" said the preacher. "Let us join together in worship! Let us give thanks for this day the Lord has made!"

They all rose to sing a hymn. "Come to the church by the wildwood," sang the whole congregation. "Oh, come to the church in the vale."

After the hymn and a prayer, and a little more organ music and some bell ringing, it was time for Sunday school.

Brother and Sister joined the other cubs as they trooped out of the chapel under the watchful eye of Preacher Brown.

Old Missus Ursula Bruinsky was the Sunday school teacher. Brother and Sister wondered just how old she was. She looked old enough to have been Mama and Papa's Sunday school teacher.

"Good morning, children," she said with a big smile. "Today we're going to learn the story of Noah's Ark." She looked around at them brightly. "Do any of you young'uns know the story of Noah's Ark?"

Cousin Fred, who read the dictionary for fun, raised his hand.

"Excellent, Fred!" said Missus Ursula. "Why don't you tell us the story?"

So Cousin Fred told the story of Noah's Ark. "Long, long ago, God saw that the people of the earth had become wicked. But Noah was a just man, and he walked with God. So God told Noah to build a great boat—an ark. God was going to bring a terrible flood upon all the earth.

And God told Noah to bring two of every sort of creature, male and female, into the ark. So Noah built the ark, gathered the animals, and went into it with his family."

Brother Bear interrupted. "Do you think they brought frogs into the ark?" he asked.

Missus Ursula laughed. "Why, I'm sure that Noah brought frogs into the ark, Brother Bear," she said, her eyes twinkling. "But if you think that you are going to bring a frog into this classroom the way your father did, young man, you have got another thing coming!"

Brother's mouth dropped wide open. Missus Ursula really was old enough to have been Mama and Papa's Sunday school teacher!

Cousin Fred went on with the story. "Then it began to rain. It rained for forty days and forty nights. All the earth was covered with the flood. And all living things, except those on the ark, died. After many months, Noah sent forth a dove. The dove came back carrying an olive leaf. Noah knew that the flood had passed. He let all of the animals go. Then God set a rainbow in the sky and promised Noah that he would never cover all the earth with the waters of a flood again."

The cubs all sighed. They were thinking back to the last big thunderstorm they'd had when the river went up over its banks and washed out the bridge. There had been a beautiful rainbow after that storm too.

"All right, cubs," said Missus Ursula. "Let's see if you can all draw pictures of the story of Noah's Ark."

There were crayons and paper on the tables, so the cubs set busily to work. Sister drew a beautiful picture of the ark resting on the mountaintop.

Brother drew a dramatic scene of rain pouring down with bolts of lightning and the ark tossing on the waves.

Too-Tall drew a picture of all the animals sticking their heads out of the ark, yelling "PEW!"

"Now, Too-Tall," said Missus Ursula. "I really don't think that's very appropriate." But Sister noticed her smiling, just the same, when she thought none of the cubs were looking.

Then, Sunday school was over. "Goodbye, cubs!" called Missus Ursula. "See you all next Sunday!"

The cubs ran outside, shouting and jumping after sitting still for so long. The grown-ups were coming out of the chapel. Preacher Brown was shaking hands with everyone, and folks were laughing and talking together.

"There!" said Mama as they headed for home. "That wasn't too bad, was it?"

"No," said Sister. "In fact, it was kind of interesting."

"Yeah," agreed Brother, running on ahead. "And now ... soccer!"

"And ballet!" added Sister.

"And football!" said Papa.

Mama rolled her eyes.

Sister began to hum, then sing softly, "Come to the church by the wildwood. Oh, come to the church in the vale."

Papa began to sing along, in rhythm, "Oh, come, come, come, come ..."

And everyone joined in, "No spot is so dear to my childhood as the little brown church in the vale!"

"YAY!" shouted Honey Bear, wanting to join in too. And they all gave her a nice round of applause.

The Berenstain Bears

The FORGIVING TREE

ZONDERVAN.com/
AUTHORTRACKER
follow your favorite authors

ZONDERkidz

Living Lights

It was a special day in a tree house down a sunny dirt road deep in Bear Country. It was Brother Bear's birthday.

"Happy Birthday, Brother!" shouted the party guests as Mama brought in the cake. Then they all sang the birthday song.

"Make a wish!" said Sister.
Brother closed his eyes, made a wish, and blew out the candles.
"YEA!" the guests yelled, clapping and blowing on noisemakers.

Papa cut the cake and everyone dug in.
"What did you wish for?" asked Cousin Fred.
"If I tell, it won't come true," said Brother.

When they were finished eating the cake, it was time to open presents. Brother got some very nice ones—a model plane, some books, a racing car set, and a video game.

Then he noticed Papa sneaking into the next room. When he came back, he was pushing ... *a brand-new bike!*

"Wow!" said Brother excitedly. "It's exactly what I wished for!"

"Lucky you didn't tell Fred," said Sister.

"That's a beautiful bike," said Fred, admiring it. "I sure wish I had a bike like that."

"Oh," said Brother, without thinking, "you can borrow it anytime you like."

"Gee, thanks!" said Fred.

"Let's try out your new video game," suggested Sister.

All the cubs crowded around while Brother and Sister played the new video game. They were so interested, they didn't notice anything else for awhile. But then Brother looked over at his brand-new bike. It was gone!

"Hey!" said Brother. "Where's my new bike?"

"Say," said Lizzy, looking out the window, "isn't that Fred riding it?"

Lizzy was right. Cousin Fred was outside riding Brother's brand-new bike around the tree house. Brother was furious!

"That Fred!" growled Brother. "He can't do that!" And he charged outside.

"Uh-oh!" said Mama and Papa, running after him.

But they were too late. Brother was already chasing Fred around the tree house yelling for him to get off his bike. He startled Fred so much that poor Fred didn't look where he was going and ran right into the mailbox.

He wasn't hurt, but the bike was. The front wheel was bent and wouldn't turn.

"Look what you did!" shouted Brother. "Who said you could ride my new bike?"

"*You* did," said Fred. "You said I could borrow it anytime."

"I didn't mean right away," said Brother, stamping his feet. "I never even got to ride it!"

"Now Brother," said Mama, "calm down. This is just a misunderstanding. Fred didn't mean any harm."

"But my bike is ruined!" cried Brother. "Just look at it!"

"It's not ruined," said Papa. "We'll take it down to the bike shop and get it fixed up as good as new."

"But it won't be new!" said Brother. "It will never be brand-new again!" And he stormed off in a huff.

"Gee, I'm sorry," said Fred. He felt awful. "I never meant to
hurt Brother or his new bike."

"Of course not, Fred," soothed Mama. "It was just an
accident."

"I'm sorry Brother's so mad," said Fred. "Do you think he'll
ever forgive me?"

"Of course he will," said Papa. "He'll get over it in no time."

But Sister wasn't so sure. She followed Brother to their backyard tree house.

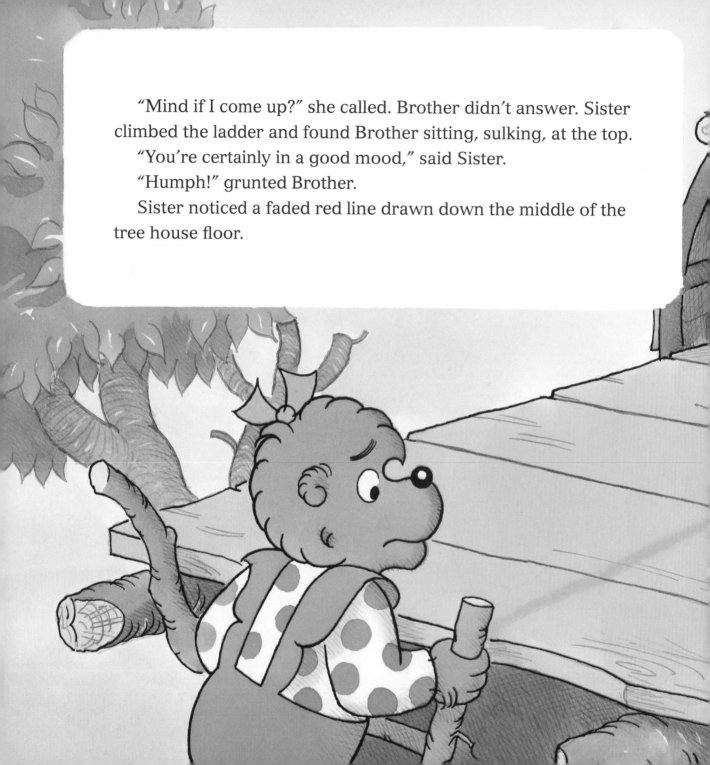

"Mind if I come up?" she called. Brother didn't answer. Sister climbed the ladder and found Brother sitting, sulking, at the top.

"You're certainly in a good mood," said Sister.

"Humph!" grunted Brother.

Sister noticed a faded red line drawn down the middle of the tree house floor.

"Do you remember this red line?" she asked.

Brother shrugged.

"We put it there a long time ago," Sister went on. "We were so mad at each other that we divided the tree house in half. I sat on one side, and you sat on the other. We sat out here being mad at each other until it started to rain and we got soaked. By that time, we couldn't even remember what we were mad about."

"I guess so," said Brother.

As Brother and Sister sat in their tree house, it became cloudy and started to rain. They went back to the party and found the guests getting ready to break the piñata.

It was one Papa made in his workshop. There were all kinds of candies inside but especially licorice because licorice was Papa's favorite. Papa held the piñata out on a broomstick.

"Okay," he said. "Start swinging. But be careful not to hit *me*!"

One after another, the cubs whacked the piñata until it finally broke open, spilling candy onto the floor.

They all scrambled to grab some, including Papa. Brother scrambled right into Fred. In fact, they knocked heads.

"Ow!" said Fred, rubbing his noggin.

"Oops, sorry!" said Brother.

"That's okay, Brother," said Fred. "I forgive you."

"I forgive you too, Fred," said Brother, feeling ashamed of himself. "I shouldn't have yelled at you about the bike. It really was just an accident."

"Forget it," said Fred … and forget it they did as they gathered up the candy.

"You know," said Papa to Mama, as they watched the happy cubs, "that old tree in the backyard has seen a lot of forgiving over the years. I guess you'd call it a Forgiving Tree."

"As the Lord said," smiled Mama: "And forgive us our debts, as we forgive our debtors."

"What does that mean?" asked Sister.

"Just that God wants us to forgive those who hurt our feelings," said Mama.

"And, remember," added Papa, "though God wants us to be good, he forgives us when we do something wrong."

"Well, I think that's very nice of God," said Sister.
"Yes," agreed Mama and Papa, "it is!"

The Berenstain Bears®
Say Their Prayers

Created by Stan and Jan Berenstain
Written by Mike Berenstain

ZONDERkidz

ZONDERVAN.com/
AUTHORTRACKER
follow your favorite authors

It was bedtime in the Bear family's tree house—
bedtime after a long, busy day. Little Honey Bear
was already asleep in her crib. Brother and Sister
were ready for bed too. They were bathed and
they had their pajamas on. Mama and Papa were
done reading them their bedtime stories. But there
was one last thing to do before they went to sleep.
It was time for Brother and Sister to kneel down
beside their bunk bed and say their prayers.

Some evenings, they added a few more blessings like "bless our friends Lizzy and Barry" or "bless Teacher Jane and Teacher Bob." But when they started adding "bless Mayor Honeypot and Police Chief Bruno," Mama and Papa decided to draw the line. Mama and Papa were falling asleep before the cubs' prayers were over.

Tonight when Mama and Papa were giving the cubs their goodnight kisses, Brother asked a question. It was a question he had been thinking about for awhile.

"Mama," he said. "Why do we say prayers before we go to sleep? I was at Barry Bruin's house for a sleepover last week, and he doesn't say prayers at all."

"Some people just don't believe in saying prayers," said Mama. "But we pray at night so we can thank God for the blessings of the day."

"Do you and Papa always say your prayers before you go to sleep?" asked Sister, half asleep in the upper bunk.

"Not exactly …" said Mama. These days Mama and Papa were so tired at bedtime that they just flopped down and were snoring almost before their heads hit the pillow. "But I think it would be a good idea if we got in the habit again." Mamma nudged Papa. "Don't you agree, Papa?"

"Huh?" he said, trying to stay awake. "Oh, right! Absolutely!"

"Good night now," said Mama. "Sweet dreams."

"Hmmm …" thought Brother, as he drifted off in the sleepy darkness. Mama's answer was okay. But he still had a few questions.

The next morning, Brother and Sister were up bright and early. It was Saturday and they had a Little League game. Their team was called the Sharks. They had a cool logo on their shirts—a big shark mouth full of sharp teeth.

"I feel hot today!" said Sister, tying her shoes. "I feel a whole lot of hits and stolen bases coming on!"

"Oh, yeah?" snorted Brother. "What about home runs? I guess I'll have to take care of that department!"

"Sure!" said Sister, punching him in the arm. "Brother Bear, the Home-Run King!" She ran, laughing, out of the room with Brother Bear chasing her. Sister and Brother liked playing on the same team. But sometimes they got just a little too competitive.

After breakfast, the whole family headed down to the ball field. Brother and Sister had practice before the game. It was Mama and Papa's turn to help with the snack bar. Papa was going to cook the hamburgers and hot dogs on the grill. Mama was going to sell candy and popcorn. Even Honey Bear would help out. It was her job to eat the leftover cotton candy. Papa soon had the grill behind the snack bar fired up. Mama opened up the candy stand, and Honey Bear started getting into the cotton candy.

The team ran out on the field for practice. Brother was playing shortstop, and Sister was at second base. Up on the mound, Cousin Fred would handle the pitching. Fred was a solid pitcher. But he had been struggling of late. His last two games were pretty shaky.

Today, they were up against the Pumas. The Pumas' uniforms weren't quite as cool as the Sharks'. But the Pumas were one of the best teams in the league. The Sharks would have their work cut out for them.

Since the Sharks were the home team, the Pumas were up first. Their lead-off batter was a big, powerful cub about twice Brother's size. He was twirling six bats around his head in the warm-up circle as if they were a bunch of twigs.

"Uh-oh!" said Brother. "Look who it is!"

Sister gulped. It was the Beast—the Pumas' best player. He could hit and field and pitch. They didn't know his real name. They just called him the Beast.

Brother glanced over at Fred on the mound. He had noticed too. He was taking off his hat to wipe his forehead. He looked pretty nervous out there.

"Play ball!" called the ump, and the game was on.

The Beast picked out a bat from his bunch and stepped into the batter's box. He took some warm-up swings and pounded his bat on the plate. He glared at Fred on the mound.

Brother noticed that Fred wasn't glaring back. In fact, he was standing quite still, his head bowed and his hands folded. It looked like his eyes were closed, and his lips seemed to be moving.

"Psst, Fred!" called Brother. "What's up?"

But Fred didn't answer. He straightened up, took a deep breath, and went into his windup. He fired a fast ball. There was a *swish* and a *thump*! The Beast had missed!

"Stee-rike one!" called the ump.

"Way to go, Freddy baby!" yelled Brother. "That's the way to pitch 'em in there! Just two more like that! You can do it!"

It was the sort of thing you always yell to encourage the pitcher. But did Brother really believe that Freddy baby could do it? It turned out that Freddy baby could.

There was another *swish*! and another *thump*! "Stee-rike two!" yelled the ump.

Another *swish* and a *thump*! "Stee-rike three!" called the ump. "Yer out!"

The batter had gone down swinging. The crowd in the stands cheered. The Beast kicked the dirt in disgust as he trudged back to the dugout.

Fred didn't look nervous anymore. Now it was the batter's turn to look nervous. Fred threw six more fast balls to two more batters. There were six *swishes* and six *thumps*. Cousin Fred had struck out the side!

"That was some pitching, Fred," said Brother later on as they sat on the bench waiting to go up to bat.

"Thanks," said Fred.

But there was something else on Brother's mind. "I was wondering, Fred," began Brother. "What were you doing out there with your head down like that?"

"Oh," shrugged Fred, a little embarrassed. "I was just praying."

"Praying?" said Brother in surprise. "What were you praying for—strikeouts?" Before Fred could answer, it was his turn to bat. He trotted out of the dugout, leaving Brother still wondering.

By the end of the game, Papa had cooked thirty-three hamburgers and forty-seven hot dogs; Mama had sold three dozen lollipops and four boxes of chocolate bars; and Honey Bear was very, very sticky.

The Sharks were in a sticky spot too. They were behind by one run with two outs and a man on base. The "man" was Sister. She had gotten to first on a walk and then stolen second—she was a feisty little player. Now it was Brother's turn to bat. If he could get a hit, the Sharks might tie it. If he got a home run, they would win.

The Pumas' pitcher was none other than the Beast. As he walked to the plate, Brother felt a little sick. Talk about pressure!

Before he stepped into the batter's box, Brother decided to do something he had never done in a baseball game. He bowed his head, closed his eyes, and said a prayer. "Dear Lord," he prayed. "Please let me get a hit."

Feeling a little more confident, Brother stepped up to the plate. The Beast wound up and let it fly. Brother didn't even see it.

"Stee-rike one!" called the ump.

Brother gripped the bat tighter. He'd get the next one. Another scorcher screamed past.

"Stee-rike two!" called the ump.

Brother clenched his teeth. He was definitely not going to let this next pitch get past him. The Beast wound up, the ball flew, and Brother swung—hard!

Swish!—Thump! "Stee-rike three!" bawled the ump. "Yer out!"

The game was over. The Sharks had lost, and Brother had struck out!

"Way to go, Home-Run King!" shouted Sister in disgust. She was angry that all her efforts to get on base had gone to waste. Brother trudged back to the dugout, his head hung low. He had never felt so awful in his life!

Later, as he packed up his things, he found Fred standing next to him. "Don't let it get to you, Brother," said Fred. "That was a tough game. The Pumas are a good team."

"Yeah," agreed Brother. "I tried everything. I even tried praying like you did when you struck out the Beast. But it didn't work for me."

"Really?" said Fred. "What did you pray for?"

"I prayed for a hit, naturally," said Brother.

"Oh," said Fred, rubbing his chin. "I see."

"Why?" asked Brother. "What did you pray for?"

"I just prayed that I wouldn't get too scared," said Fred simply.

Brother blinked at him. "I guess your prayer was answered!"

"Prayers are always answered," said Fred. "Sometimes, we just don't get the answer we expect. Say," he added, sniffing the air. "Do you smell something burning?"

That's when they noticed the column of thick black smoke rising from behind the stands. "The snack bar!" they both yelled, and ran for it.

The smoke was coming from a batch of burning hot dogs on the grill. Papa was covered with soot and was trying to put the fire out with his hat. Mama came running up with a fire extinguisher. A few good squirts and the flames were under control. Honey Bear was laughing and clapping.

"Boy!" coughed Fred, waving the smoke away. "Maybe we should have prayed for rain!"

That evening at bedtime, Brother and Sister knelt down beside their bunk bed to say their prayers. Tonight, they felt like a nice long one:

"Bless Mama, bless Papa, bless Honey Bear, bless Grizzly Gramps, bless Grizzly Gran, bless Cousin Fred, Uncle Willie, and Aunt Min. Bless our friends Lizzie and Barry, and bless Teacher Bob, and ..."

When they were finished, Brother and Sister woke Mama and Papa up and climbed into bed. Mama and Papa kissed them goodnight, turned out the light, and went downstairs.

As Brother lay drowsily in his bed, he started thinking over the day's baseball game. If only he had been able to get that hit … or even a home run!

"That was a tough game today, wasn't it?" he said to Sister up on the top bunk.

"Yeah," answered Sister. "Tough on you, Mr. Strike-Out King."

"What's that supposed to mean?" said Brother, glaring up at the bottom of her bunk. "I played my best! A strike out like that could happen to anybody!"

But Sister didn't answer. She was fast asleep. Brother rolled over and ground his teeth. Sometimes Sister Bear made him so angry he could just … But then he thought of something. He thought of another prayer.

"Dear God," he prayed. "Please help me out with my little sister!" And to his surprise, he found his prayer had been answered. He didn't feel angry anymore.

"Thanks for the help up there!" he said.
And with a sigh, he fell asleep.

The Berenstain Bears.
Faithful Friends

Living Lights™

written by Jan and Mike Berenstain

ZONDERVAN.com/
AUTHORTRACKER
follow your favorite authors

ZONDERkidz

Lizzy Bruin was Sister Bear's very best friend. It seemed like they had been best friends for a very long time.

Lizzy Bruin and Sister Bear had been through a lot together. Once they had a slumber party that got a little out of hand.

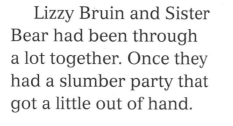

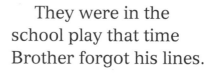

They were in the school play that time Brother forgot his lines.

They built their own clubhouse when Brother kept them out of his.

They played dress up
and dolls, and rode their
bikes, and picked flowers,
and rolled down hills, and
giggled.

Sister was glad she had such a good friend. She could always rely on Lizzy to be there for her. They hardly ever fought or argued. Not, that is, until Sister started to spend more time with Suzy MacGrizzie.

Suzy was a new cub in town. At first, Sister and her friends didn't pay much attention to Suzy. But then, Sister noticed how lonely Suzy was and invited her to play. From then on, Suzy was part of Sister's little group.

All of Sister's friends, including Lizzy, liked Suzy. She was one more cub to spend time with and enjoy.

But Suzy was a little different from the other cubs. For one thing, she read an awful lot. And she was interested in different things—science, for instance. Suzy invited Sister over one night to look at the sky. Suzy pointed her telescope up at the moon.

"Wow!" said Sister, looking into the eyepiece. "It looks so close." She could actually see mountains and valleys and craters on the moon. It was very interesting.

One day, Suzy asked Sister to go on a butterfly hunt with her. They took butterfly nets and went out into the fields.

Sister caught a big yellow butterfly with black stripes. Suzy caught one that had bright red and blue spots on it and long swallowtails. It was very beautiful. After they studied the butterflies for a while, they let them go, and the butterflies sailed up into the sky over the trees.

"They're so pretty!" said Sister.

On their way back, Suzy and Sister ran into Lizzy and their friends Anna and Millie. They were all carrying their Bearbie dolls. "Hiya, gang!" called Sister when she saw them. "Suzy and I were out catching butterflies. You should have seen the big yellow one I got!"

"Yeah, great," said Lizzy. "Well, see you, I guess."
"Wait a minute," said Sister. "Where are you all going?"
"We're going over to my garage to play Bearbie dolls," said Lizzy.
"Can Suzy and I come too?" asked Sister.

"It looks like you two are already pretty busy," said Lizzy. "Come on, girls." With that, Lizzy and her friends went on their way.

"How do you like that?" said Sister, hurt and angry. "Who does she think she is? Come on, Suzy, we'll play over at my house. Who needs them, anyway?"

When they got to the Bear family's tree house, Suzy and Sister found Brother Bear and Cousin Fred getting out their fishing tackle.

"Lizzy and your friends were here looking for you," Brother said. "I told them you were playing with Suzy. Lizzy didn't seem very happy."

"That Lizzy Bruin!" said Sister, annoyed. "What business is it of hers who I play with?"

"I guess she's jealous," said Brother.

"Jealous?" said Sister, puzzled.

"Sure," said Brother. "She's been your best friend for years. You mean a lot to her. She's just worried that maybe you don't like her as much as you used to."

"Oh," said Sister, "that's silly!" It was true that she liked her new friend, Suzy. But Lizzy would always be her best friend.

"What should I do?" Sister wondered.

Cousin Fred spoke up. "You know what the Bible says: 'Wounds from a friend can be trusted.'" Fred liked to memorize things.

"Huh?" said both Sister and Brother. "What does that mean?"

Suzy answered—she liked to memorize things too. "I think it means that when a friend who loves you hurts your feelings, you need to find out what is bothering her."

"Yes," Fred nodded. "And the Bible also says that we shouldn't stay angry with our friends. God wants us to make up with them if we have an argument."

"Oh," said Sister, thoughtfully.

"I have an idea," said Brother. "Fred and I were about to go fishing. Why don't we grab some extra fishing gear and go over to Lizzy's? We can see if they would all like to go fishing with us."

"Great!" said Sister. Suzy grinned.

So they all stopped by Lizzy's garage on their way to the fishing hole.

"Hey, Lizzy!" called Sister. "Do you and Anna and Millie want to go fishing with us?"

Lizzy acted like she wasn't so sure. But Anna and Millie were all for it, and Lizzy certainly didn't want to be left out.

Soon, they were all down at the fishing hole. Lizzy cast her line out into the middle of the pond and got her line into a terrible tangle.

"Here, let me help you, Lizzy," said Sister, taking her fishing rod. "I'll untangle it for you."

"Wow, thanks!" said Lizzy. "You're a real friend, Sister."

"I always have been and I always will be!" said Sister, giving Lizzy a hug.

And together they picked away at the tangled fishing line.

The Berenstain Bears®

Show Some
Respect

written by
Jan and Mike Berenstain

Living
Lights™

ZONDERVAN.com/
AUTHORTRACKER
follow your favorite authors

ZONDERkidz

It was a beautiful summer morning and the Bear family was going on a picnic. Mama and Papa packed up the picnic things. Brother, Sister, and Honey were very excited. Grizzly Gramps and Gran were coming too.

"I made a pot of my special wilderness stew for the picnic," said Gran. "Mmm-mmm!" said Gramps. "Wilderness stew—my favorite!" "Yuck-o!" muttered Brother. "Wilderness stew—not one of my favorites."

Sister laughed.

"What was that, Brother?" asked Mama.

"Oh, nothing, Mama," said Brother. "Come on, Sis. Let's pick out a good picnic spot."

The family headed down the sunny dirt road
to find the perfect spot for their picnic. Sister and
Brother ran on ahead.

"Wait for us please, cubs," said Mama. But Sister
and Brother paid no attention.

"Hmmm …," said Mama, none too pleased.

"I remember a good picnic spot right in these trees," said Papa. "We used to come here when I was in school."

"That was about a hundred years ago," said Sister.
"It's pretty run down now. Let's find a better spot."
"Hmmm!" said Papa, none too pleased.

"I know a lovely spot down by that pond," said Mama. "Papa and I came here on our first date."

"That was an awful long time ago," said Brother. "It's full of mosquitoes now. Let's find a better spot."

"Hmmm!" said Mama and Papa, none too pleased.

"I recall a time when Gramps and I had a nice picnic on top of Big Bear Hill," said Gran as they went on their way. "There was a lovely view, and …"

"Now, Gran," interrupted Mama. "We don't want to climb all the way up Big Bear Hill. Let's find a better spot."

"Hmmm!" said Gran, none too pleased.

The Bear family trudged across the countryside. They were getting hungry, hot, and tired.

"I have a good idea for a picnic spot," said Gramps. "How about we all …"

"Now, Gramps," interrupted Papa. "We don't need any help—we know what we're doing."

Gramps stopped short.

"Now, just a doggone minute!" he said. "It seems to me that you folks aren't showing much respect for your elders."

"That's right," agreed Gran. "Brother and Sister are being disrespectful to Mama and Papa."

"And Mama and Papa are being disrespectful to you and me," added Gramps. "You know, us old folks know a thing or two. As the Bible says, 'Age should speak; advanced years should teach wisdom.'"

"But, Gramps!" said Papa.

"But me no 'buts,' sonny!" said Gramps. "'A wise son heeds his father's instruction,'" he added, quoting the Bible, again.

"Sonny?" said Brother and Sister. It never occurred to them that Papa was someone's "sonny."

When they thought it over, Brother, Sister, Mama, and Papa realized that Gramps and Gran were right. They were being disrespectful.

"We're sorry!" said Brother and Sister. "We were excited about the picnic and forgot our manners. We'll be sure to show more respect from now on."

"And we're sorry too!" said Mama and Papa. "We know we shouldn't speak to our elders that way."

"That's fine," smiled Gran. "All is forgiven. Now come along. Gramps will pick a good picnic-spot for us. He's Bear Country's foremost picnic-spot picker-outer."

"Yes, indeedy," said Gramps. "Besides, if we leave it up to all of you, we might starve!"

"Where are we going, Gramps?" asked Brother and Sister as Gramps led them across the countryside. "Never fear," said Gramps. "Grizzly Gramps, the picnic-spot picker-outer, is here!"

They marched over hill and dale, through wood and field.
"Now there's the perfect picnic spot!" said Gramps, at last.
"But, Gramps!" said Sister. "That's your own house."

"That's right, young'un," he smiled. "Didn't you ever hear of a backyard picnic?"

Gramps and Papa got the grill fired up and they added honey grilled salmon to Gran's wilderness stew.

"Mmm-mmm!" said Brother and Sister. "Honey grilled salmon—that's our favorite!"

They raised glasses of lemonade to Grizzly Gramps, the eldest member of the family.

"To Grizzly Gramps," said Papa, "Bear Country's best picnic-spot picker-outer!"

"You know," said Gramps, as he dug into a big helping of wilderness stew, "it's about time I got a little respect around here."

The Berenstain Bears®
KINDNESS COUNTS

written by Jan and Mike Berenstain

ZONDERVAN.com/
AUTHORTRACKER
follow your favorite authors

ZONDERk*dz

Living
Lights™

Brother Bear was a bear of many interests. He enjoyed sports such as baseball, soccer, football, and basketball. He liked to draw and paint, and he was interested in science. He had hobbies like collecting stamps and baseball cards, and he enjoyed fishing and playing video games. But the thing he enjoyed most of all was building model airplanes.

He started building models with Papa when he was very young.
At first, they made simple plastic models. But, soon, they were
creating flying models out of lightweight wood and paper. Before
long, Brother could build models all by himself.

He kept building bigger and better models that could fly longer, farther, and higher. On trips to the park with Sister Bear, he always took along his latest model for flight trials. It was a thrill to wind its propeller for the first time, let it go, and watch it fly across the park.

One Saturday afternoon, Brother tried out his latest creation, a big model plane painted bright red called *The Meteor*. He set it down on the grass and wound the propeller. Sister joined some of her friends nearby. One of them was minding her younger brother, Billy. He was playing with a small model plane like the ones Brother had when he was little.

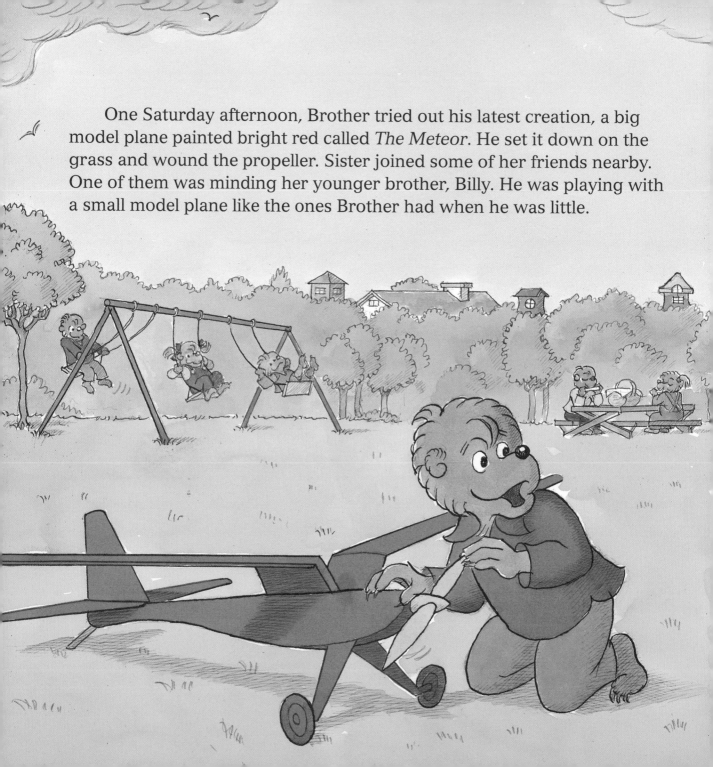

When Billy saw Brother's big new plane, he came over to take a look.

"Wow!" he said. "That's beautiful!"

"Thanks! She's called *The Meteor*. I built her myself," Brother said proudly.

"Wow!" said Billy. "I wish I could build a plane like that."

Brother finished winding the propeller and picked up *The Meteor*.
"Can I help you fly it?" asked Billy.

Brother was proud of his models and careful with them too. They took a long time to build and were easy to break. If you didn't launch them just right, they could take a nosedive and crash.

"Well," said Brother doubtfully, "I don't know...," But he remembered how Papa always let him help out when they were building and flying model planes. That's how he learned—by helping Papa.

"Well," said Brother, "okay. You can help me hold it."

"Oh, boy! Thanks!" said Billy.

Brother knelt down and let Billy hold the model with him.

"Now, remember," said Brother, "don't throw it—let it fly out of your hands. Here we go—one, two, three ... *fly!*"

They both let go, and the big red *Meteor* lifted up and away, its propeller whirring.

"YIPEEE!" yelled Billy. "Look at it fly!"

But Brother was worried. *The Meteor* was climbing up too steeply. As they watched, *The Meteor* rose high above the park. It seemed to pause in midair. Its nose suddenly dipped down, and it went into a dive. *The Meteor* hit the ground with a nasty *crunch*!

Brother and Billy ran to the wrecked model. Brother sadly picked it up and looked at the damage. Billy's big sister and the others noticed the excitement and came over.

"Oh, no!" said Billy. "Is it my fault? Did I do something wrong? Did I throw it instead of letting it fly like you said?"

Brother shook his head. "Of course not!" he said. "You did fine. This is my fault. I didn't get the balance right. It's tail heavy. That's why it went up too steep, paused, and dove down. That's called 'stalling.'"

"Are you going to fix it?" asked Billy.

"Sure!" laughed Brother. "'Build 'em, fly 'em, crash 'em, fix 'em!' That's my motto."

"Could I help you?" wondered Billy.

"Now, Billy," said his big sister, "you're too young to help."

But Brother remembered how Papa always
used to let him help. That was how he learned
about model airplanes.

"That's okay," Brother told Billy's big sister.
"I don't mind. I could use a little help."

So Billy came along to the Bears' tree house. Mama and Papa were pleased that Brother was being so kind to young Billy.

"It's just as the Good Book says," Mama said, "'Blessed are the merciful, for they will be shown mercy.'"

"Yes," agreed Papa, "and it also says in the Bible that a kind person benefits himself."

"What does that mean?" wondered Brother.

"It means that no act of kindness is wasted," said Papa. "Any kindness you do will always come back to you."

Blessed are
the merciful,
for they will
be shown
mercy.
Matthew 5:7

Every afternoon that week, Billy helped Brother work on the plane. He didn't know very much, but he learned a lot and he had lots of fun. Brother had fun too. He enjoyed teaching, and he liked having a helper who looked up to him.

The next Saturday, *The Meteor* was ready for another flight. Brother and Billy took it down to the park. Everyone came along to watch. They wound *The Meteor's* propeller, held it up, and let it fly. It lifted away and rose in a long, even curve.

"This looks like a good flight!" said Brother.

The Meteor flew on and on across the field. Slowly, it came down, landing clear on the other side of the park in a three-point landing. Brother and Billy ran over. It was in perfect shape.

"Hurray!" yelled Billy, jumping up and down.

Brother began to wind up the propeller for another try, but he noticed a group of older cubs coming into the park. They carried a lot of interesting equipment and wore jackets that said "Bear Country Rocket Club." Brother went over to watch. They were setting up a model rocket. They were going to fire it off and let it come down by parachute. Brother was excited.

"Excuse me," he said to the cub in charge, "do you think I could help you launch the rocket?"

The cub shook his head. "Sorry!" he said. "You're too young. It's too dangerous."

Brother walked away sadly. But he noticed that Billy was staying behind. He was talking to the older cub in charge. The older cub called Brother back.

"My cousin, Billy, tells me you let him help with your model plane," said the older cub. Brother just nodded. The older cub smiled. "That was cool. You seem to know a lot about flying and models. I guess you can help out."

So the rocket club let Brother hold things for them, carry things for them, and squirt a little glue here and there. He learned a lot and he was happy. When it was time to fire off the rocket, they even let Brother push the button.

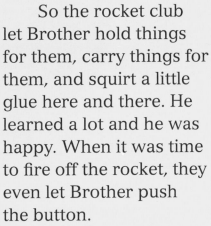

"10, 9, 8, 7, 6, 5, 4, 3, 2, 1 ... *fire!*" said the cub in charge, and Brother pushed the button.

There was a loud *WHOOOSH*!

The rocket shot up, leaving a trail of smoke.

High above the park a yellow parachute popped open, and the rocket drifted back to earth.

They ran over to it. It was all twisted and scorched.

"Are you going to fix it?" asked Brother.

"Sure," laughed the older cub. "'Build 'em, fly 'em, crash 'em, fix 'em!' That's our motto."

"Could I help you?" asked Brother.

The older cub thought it over. "Sure," he said, slapping Brother on the back. "Why not?"

So, because Brother Bear had shown a little kindness to someone younger than himself, he became the youngest member, ever, of the Bear Country Rocket Club.

And was he ever proud!

The Berenstain Bears®
and A Job Well Done

written by
Jan and Mike Berenstain

ZONDERVAN.com/
AUTHORTRACKER
follow your favorite authors

ZONDERkidz

Living
Lights™

It was spring in Bear Country. And that meant that it was
spring cleaning and fix-up time at the Bear family's tree house.
Mama, Papa, Brother, Sister, and even Honey all had jobs to do.

Mama and Papa got right down to work. Mama hung up rugs on the line to beat the dirt out of them. Papa started to fix the broken railing on the front steps.

Brother and Sister had a job too. They were supposed to clean up the old playhouse in the backyard. Honey was going to help them.

They all got off to a good start. The sun was shining, and the air was fresh and clean. Birds were singing, and bright flowers were blooming in the garden.

Mama whacked at the rugs. Huge clouds of dirt flew out of them.

Papa's tools were everywhere. He knelt down to carve a piece of wood into the right shape for the railing.

Brother, Sister, and Honey had everything they needed for their job. They had brooms and brushes, cloths and mops, buckets of hot water and lots of soap. First, they were going to sweep out the inside of the playhouse.

"Uh-oh!" said Brother, looking
inside the playhouse. "Spiders!"
    Sister and Honey peeked inside.
Sure enough, there were some big,
hairy spiders sitting in their webs up in
the corners of the playhouse. Brother,
Sister, and Honey hated spiders!
    "Yuck!" they all said.
    "What should we do?" asked Sister.

"Let's not sweep out the inside," said Brother. "Let's scrub the outside. Maybe that will scare the spiders out."

That's what they did. Brother worked his way around the playhouse with his scrub brush, whistling while he worked.

"Hey, look!" he said when he got to the back. "We left some baseball stuff out here."

There was an old baseball, a bat, and a glove behind the playhouse.

Brother picked up the ball, tossed it in the air, and caught it. Sister picked up the bat and gave it a few swings.

"Pitch it in!" she said to Brother.

Brother wound up and tossed the ball to Sister. She swatted it across the lawn.

"Here, Honey," said Brother, giving her the glove. "You be the outfielder."

Honey toddled out into the lawn and sat down.

Meanwhile, back at the tree house, Mama and Papa were hard at work. Mama was nearly done with the rugs. She was absolutely covered with dirt.

Papa was nearly finished with the railing. He fastened the wood in place, then straightened up and stretched.

That's when Papa noticed
Honey sitting in the middle
of the lawn. He couldn't see
Brother or Sister. They were
behind the tree house.
    "What is Honey
doing just sitting there?"
wondered Papa.

A baseball came sailing into sight and landed near Honey. She grabbed it and threw it back.

"Hmmm!" said Papa, rubbing his chin.

Papa walked around the tree
house and saw Brother and Sister
playing baseball. Their brooms,
brushes, cloths, and mops were all
lying on the ground.

Papa stood behind Brother and Sister.

"Baseball is a fine springtime activity," he said, "but so is spring cleaning!"

Brother and Sister spun around and hid the ball and bat behind their backs.

"Oh, hi, Papa!" they both grinned. "We were just taking a little break."

Papa looked into the very dirty playhouse.

"It looks like you've been taking a *big* break," he said. "You've hardly touched this playhouse."

"But Papa," started Brother.

"There are lots of spiders in there!" finished Sister.

Papa smiled. He remembered how scared he was of spiders when he was a cub. He still didn't like them very much. "Well," he said, "I'll chase the spiders out for you. But, then, you need to get the job done."

Papa chased the spiders out of the playhouse with a broom. They ran off and hid in the storage shed, which was a better home for them, anyway.

Then, Brother, Sister, and Honey went back to work.

"Did you know that the Bible has something to say about working hard and getting the job done?" asked Papa as they cleaned.

"No," said Brother.

"What does it say?" said Sister.

"It says," said Papa, "'finish your outdoor work and get your fields ready; after that, build your house.'"

"Did you build a house today, Papa?" asked Sister.

"Well," said Papa, proudly, "I built a new railing."

"And," added Mama, who had come up to see what was going on, "it says in the Bible that God made work for us to do and there's nothing better than to enjoy your work."

"Did you enjoy your work, Mama?" asked Brother.
Mama rubbed some of the dirt off her face. "Well," she said, "I enjoy my clean rugs—and you will enjoy your clean playhouse."

"Especially without all those spiders!" agreed Sister.
"Yuck!" said Honey.
Mama, Papa, Brother, and Sister all laughed.

The Berenstain Bears. and the Golden Rule

Activities and Questions from Brother and Sister Bear

Talk about it:

1. When has someone treated you in a way you didn't like?

2. When have you treated someone in a way that wasn't very kind or fair?

Get out and do it:

1. Cut out a large construction paper heart. Write the golden rule on it and hang it on your bedroom wall.

2. Use chalk to draw a hopscotch frame on the driveway or sidewalk. Invite a friend to play with you.

3. Do something kind and unexpected for someone in your family.

The Berenstain Bears.
Go to Sunday School

Activities and Questions from Brother and Sister Bear

Talk about it:

1. How is the Bear family's church different from yours? How is it the same?

2. What are some things your family does on Sundays?

Get out and do it:

1. Draw or paint a scene from a favorite Bible story, or use magazine pictures to make a collage.

2. Draw and label four things you like about Sunday school.

The Berenstain Bears

THE FORGIVING TREE

Activities and Questions from Brother and Sister Bear

Talk about it:

1. Would you have done the same thing as Brother and offered to share your bike with Cousin Fred? Why?

2. Would you have been as upset as Brother if someone that you care about had an accident with something that was yours? What might you do differently?

3. How was Sister a help to Brother?

4. Why is it sometimes very hard to say you are sorry and also hard to accept an apology?

Get out and do it:

1. On a large sheet of butcher paper, design a Family Forgiving Tree. Have an envelope filled with cut-outs of leaves near where you hang the tree. When you need to say you are sorry to someone, write about it on a leaf and tape it to the tree. It feels good to ask for forgiveness and to be forgiven!

The Berenstain Bears.
Say Their Prayers

Activities and Questions from Brother and Sister Bear

Talk about it:

1. What did Fred mean when he said, "Prayers are always answered. Sometimes we just don't get the answer we expect"?

2. How do you think Brother's prayer at the end of the book helped him with the problem he had with his sister?

Get out and do it:

1. Design a cool shirt for a sports team called the Bears.

2. Visit a park with a baseball field. Run around the bases. Name something you are good at or thankful for at each base.

3. Make up and memorize a prayer for bedtime. Say it every night before you go to bed.

The Berenstain Bears.
Faithful Friends

Activities and Questions from Brother and Sister Bear

Talk about it:

1. How can you invite new friends into your friend group?

2. Have you ever felt left out by a friend? What do you think God would want you to do when that happens?

3. Do you like to do different things with different friends? Name some things you do differently.

Get out and do it:

1. Design a constellation—a group of stars that make a picture. Tape a piece of black paper over the end of an empty toilet paper tube. Use a pin to poke holes in the paper in a design. Look through the tube at a light to see your constellation design.

2. Draw a fish outline. Fill the outline with crayon textures, cut paper, and other materials to create eyes, mouth, and textured scales and fins.

3. Play Follow the Leader. Take turns being the leader.

The Berenstain Bears.

Show Some Respect

Activities and Questions from Brother and Sister Bear

Talk about it:

1. What does "respect others" mean? To whom should we show respect? Do we only have to show respect to those older than we are?

2. Have you ever felt that someone did not give you respect that you deserved? How did that make you feel? Did you talk about it with that person?

3. Which of God's Ten Commandments talk about respect? Explain.

Get out and do it:

Show respect to people in your community. There are many ways!

a) Make cards for the elderly or sick in your church family and take them to the hospital or nursing home.
b) Organize a group of friends to rake leaves, cut grass, or do yard clean-up for people in your neighborhood.
c) Organize a food drive or blanket collection for those in your larger community that are less fortunate than you. Deliver the items to a local shelter or take to your church for distribution.

The Berenstain Bears.
Kindness Counts

Activities and Questions from Brother and Sister Bear

Talk about it:

1. Do you have a special talent or hobby? How did you first become interested in this hobby? How did Brother become interested in model airplanes?

2. Why did Brother hesitate before actually sharing his model airplane with Billy? Why is it sometimes difficult to share something you really like and other times very easy?

3. Describe a time that you have shown kindness to someone and been shown a kindness in return. Do you think that you need to be rewarded every time you do something nice? Why or why not?

Get out and do it:

1. Create a poster for your family to hang in a prominent place in the house. Have the following scripture phrase on it: "In everything, do to others what you would want them to do to you." (Matthew 7:12)

2. Organize a family hobby day. Have each family member share what they enjoy doing the most with the rest of the family. Remember to be kind as you explain directions and show others your hobby.

The Berenstain Bears and A Job Well Done

Activities and Questions from Brother and Sister Bear

Talk about it:

1. Do you have at-home jobs that need to get done before you can have some fun? Name some of the chores you do and how it helps the family when you finish them completely.

2. What do you think Papa Bear meant when he said the Bible says, "finish your outdoor work and get your fields ready; after that, build your house?"

Get out and do it:

1. Design a family chore chart. Hang the chart up and check it daily, making sure you are completing your family responsibilities.

2. Help someone in your family with one of their given jobs around the house. Do not wait to be asked!

The Berenstain Bears®

Living Lights™

9780310712503
$3.99

9780310712497
$3.99

9780310712527
$3.99

9780310712565
$3.99

9780310720898
$3.99

9780310722861
$3.99

9780310720904
$3.99

A Lift the Flap Book
9780310720812
$6.99

A Lift the Flap Book
9780310720836
$6.99

Stickers Included
9780310720850
$4.99

Stickers Included
9780310720881
$4.99

ZONDERkidz™
.com

The Berenstain Bears®

Living Lights™

Bind-ups

5 Books in 1
9780310720102
$10.99

5 Books in 1
9780310725916
$10.99

3 Books in 1
9780310734925
$7.99

3 Books in 1
9780310735038
$7.99

Hardcover Titles

9780310719366
$6.99

9780310719373
$6.99

9780310719380
$6.99

9780310719397
$6.99

9780310722762
$6.99

9780310727149
$6.99

9780310722779
$6.99

9780310727132
$6.99

ZONDERkidz™
.com